FIFTY FOR FLUTE

Fifty progressive studies for unaccompanied flute

BOOK II

ALAN BULLARD

ABRSM

Published by ABRSM (Publishing) Ltd, a wholly owned subsidiary of ABRSM
Printed in England by Caligraving Ltd, Thetford, Norfolk, on materials from sustainable sources
Reprinted in 2019

PREFACE

The fifty short unaccompanied pieces in these two books explore the versatility of the flute and the many moods and styles it can portray. From 'Rag-time flute' to 'Spooky flute' and from 'Dreamy flute' to 'Furious flute', every one has its own character, and I hope that the titles will help the performer to create an individual mood for each.

The pieces have been designed primarily as studies but may be grouped as desired into suites for solo performance. The material has been arranged in progressive order of difficulty, with Book I covering a level of Grades 1 to 5 and Book II covering Grades 6 to 8.

All metronome marks are given as a guide only.

I would like to thank the many flute teachers and pupils who have tried these pieces out for their helpful comments and suggestions.

ALAN BULLARD

Book I

1.	Holiday flute	*page* 3
2.	Sad flute	4
3.	Restful flute	4
4.	Hungarian flute	5
5.	Bouncy flute	5
6.	Crotchety flute	6
7.	Marching flute	6
8.	Nimble flute	7
9.	Echo flute	8
10.	Dancing flute	8
11.	Ambushed flute	9
12.	Melancholy flute	10
13.	Gracious flute	10
14.	Soldier flute	11
15.	Lop-sided flute	11
16.	Romantic flute	12
17.	Cool flute	12
18.	Cheerful flute	13
19.	Neat-fingered flute	14
20.	Dreamy flute	15
21.	Plaintive flute	15
22.	Rag-time flute	16
23.	Latin flute	17
24.	Unhappy flute	18
25.	Twopenny flute	18
26.	Playful flute	20
27.	Grumpy flute	21
28.	Victorian flute	*page* 22
29.	Thoughtful flute	23
30.	Baroque flute	24

Book II

31.	Swung flute	3
32.	Blue flute	4
33.	Spanish flute	5
34.	Seafaring flute	6
35.	Comical flute	6
36.	Circus flute	8
37.	Military flute	9
38.	Stomping flute	10
39.	Waltzing flute	11
40.	Spooky flute	12
41.	Happy flute	12
42.	Solitary flute	14
43.	Flippant flute	14
44.	Furious flute	16
45.	Lively flute	17
46.	Fluent flute	18
47.	Agile flute	18
48.	Reflective flute	20
49.	Breathless flute	20
50.	Pastoral flute	22

FIFTY FOR FLUTE

BOOK II

ALAN BULLARD

31. Swung flute

32. Blue flute

33. Spanish flute

34. Seafaring flute

Con brio (𝅗𝅥 = *c.*126)

35. Comical flute

Allegro leggiero (𝅗𝅥 = *c.*144)

poco accel. al fine

36. Circus flute

Allegretto con brio (♩ = c.92)

37. Military flute

Andante ritmico (♩ = c.96)

38. Stomping flute

39. Waltzing flute

40. Spooky flute

41. Happy flute

9
13
17
f
21
mf
f
25
f
29
32
ff
f
35
mf
39
p
tr
ff

42. Solitary flute

43. Flippant flute

mf
f
mf
p
pp
f
p
mf
f
mf
f
ff
fp
pp

44. Furious flute

Originally published in *Woodwind World 5* (Trinity College, London), and used with permission.

45. Lively flute

Allegro con spirito (♩ = c.112)

46. Fluent flute

Allegro non troppo (𝅗𝅥. = *c.*116)

47. Agile flute

Con brio (𝅗𝅥 = *c.*126)

rit.

48. Reflective flute

49. Breathless flute

ossia
flutter
ossia
flutter

50. Pastoral flute

Andante improvisando
con molto rubato